Shimmer and Shine™

Backyard Ballet

Adapted by Mary Tillworth
Based on the teleplay "Backyard Ballet" by Lacey Dyer
Illustrated by Liana Hee

A GOLDEN BOOK • NEW YORK

T#: 433547
randomhousekids.com
ISBN 978-0-553-52202-0
Printed in the United States of America
10 9 8 7 6 5

Leah and Zac were twirling and leaping around Leah's living room. They had just seen *Swan Lake*, and they were practicing to put on their own ballet!

Leah spun and lost her balance. Zac crashed into the couch!

"I guess we need more practice," Leah giggled.

Zac grinned. "How about you practice spinning and I practice leaping? Later we can dance *Swan Lake* together!"

After Zac left to practice on his own, Leah sighed.
"If only I could dance like the real Swan Queen."
Suddenly, she had an idea!

Leah summoned Shimmer and Shine, twin genies-in-training who could grant her three wishes a day.

"I wish I was the Swan Queen!" Leah declared.

"*Boom, Zahramay!* First wish of the day!" chanted Shine.

Leah found herself dressed as the Swan Queen from the ballet—but with six loud swans as royal subjects!

"I was hoping to spin like the *ballerina* Swan Queen, not be the actual queen of six swans!" she said.

Shine frowned. "Oh, sounds like I made a mistake."

Leah smiled. "It's okay, Shine. Sometimes mistakes happen. Maybe these swans won't get in the way of spinning practice!"

But having six swans in Leah's living room
turned into a giant honking disaster!

Leah had to get the swans outside before they destroyed the whole house.

"I wish the swans would follow me!" she cried. Shimmer jangled her magic bracelets. "*Boom, Zahramay! Second wish of the day!*"

Now the swans followed Leah's every move,
whether she turned her head or hopped on one foot.
Though it wasn't what she had wished for, she loved it!
The swans lined up and followed her to the backyard.

Leah had saved her home from the swans, but she had forgotten to practice for the ballet performance!

She closed her eyes and made her final wish.
"I wish to be a ballerina in *Swan Lake*!"

When Leah opened her eyes, she was standing on a rock, surrounded by lily pads. Her backyard had been transformed into a giant lake!

She looked around. "This is beautiful, but I wanted to dance like the ballerina from *Swan Lake*, not have an actual lake."

Shine hung her head. "Sorry, Leah. I didn't mean to make such a big mistake."

Leah hugged Shine. "It's okay. No mistake is too big to fix. Even one as big as a lake!"

Leah started to inch off the rock. "Let's get back to dry land so we can practice spinning!" Suddenly, she slipped!

As Leah fell, she bounced off a lily pad and did a perfect ballerina spin!

"I don't know if you meant to do that, but it was amazing!" said Shine.

Leah kept bouncing and spinning from pad to pad. The swans did the same.

"If I practice more," she said, "maybe I'll finally spin like the Swan Queen!"

For the rest of the afternoon, Leah, the genies, and the swans practiced ballet on the lily pads.

Late in the day, Zac poked his head through a loose board in the fence. Shimmer and Shine quickly hid, but he didn't even notice them.

"Whoa!" he shouted to Leah. "There's a lake in your backyard!"

Zac had been practicing his leaps and was
ready for the show. "You've got everything we need—
the swans, the Swan Lake, and the Swan Queen!"

"I'm still missing one more piece." Leah held out her hand. "The best leaper ever! Wanna dance?"

Together the two friends put on a magical performance!

After the show, Leah found Shimmer and Shine.
"We fixed our mistakes, and the day turned out great!"
She hugged the two genies. "See you tomorrow?"

"Abso-*genie*-lutely!" chimed Shimmer and Shine.